CHICO BON BON
MONKEY WITH A TOOL BELT

THE PIZZA PROBLEM!

Adapted by Patty Michaels
Based on the episode written by Michael Goldberg
Based on the TV show
Chico Bon Bon: Monkey with a Tool Belt

Ready-to-Read

Simon Spotlight
New York London Toronto Sydney New Delhi

SIMON SPOTLIGHT

An imprint of Simon & Schuster Children's Publishing Division
1230 Avenue of the Americas, New York, New York 10020
This Simon Spotlight edition September 2021
CHICO BON BON™ MONKEY WITH A TOOL BELT™ Chico Bon Bon:
Monkey with a Tool Belt Copyright © 2021 Monkey WTB Limited,
a Silvergate Media company. All rights reserved.

Manufactured in the United States of America 0821 LAK
2 4 6 8 10 9 7 5 3 1
ISBN 978-1-5344-9740-5 (hc)
ISBN 978-1-5344-9739-9 (pbk)
ISBN 978-1-5344-9741-2 (ebook)

It was a sunny day
at Bon Bon Labs.

Chico Bon Bon spotted something flying in the air.

"Is it a bird?
Is it a plane?"
Rainbow Thunder
asked.

"No, it is *Super* Tiny!" Chico said.

"Is Tiny flying?"
Clark asked.

"He is! Tiny is flying by using science!" Rainbow Thunder said.

"We are using air pressure
(say: preh-SHUR)
to hold up Tiny."

"The air pressure comes from the air coming out of the Bon Bon leaf blower," Chico said.

Just then
the banana phone rang.

"Chico Bon Bon here. Got a problem? We can solve 'em!" Chico answered.

"Hi, Chico!"
Mr. McFluster
(say: muk-FLUH-stir) said.
"I have a pizza problem!
Can you help me?"

"We will be there soon!"
Chico said. "Fix-It Force,
it is time to bring
the awesome!"

The Fix-It Force met
Mr. McFluster at
Bridgeless Canyon.

"I cannot get this pizza over the canyon to Herb the Hermit Crab," Mr. McFluster said.

"You are in luck!
I can use the pie-flyer,"
Chico said.

"Or I can fly the
Clark-copter!" Clark said.
"And I can use my
glitter cycle,"
Rainbow Thunder added.

"Pie-throwing and
vehicles are
not allowed,"
Mr. McFluster said.

The Fix-It Force
decided to build a bridge.

But suddenly the bridge
was eaten by beetles!

Chico took a banana break to think of a solution.

"I wish Super Tiny could fly the pizza there," Chico said.

Just then Chico had an idea. They could use air pressure!

"If we set up leaf blowers, Mr. McFluster can float across the canyon in the air!" Rainbow Thunder said.

The Fix-It Force
collected leaf blowers
and set them up at
full power.

Mr. McFluster made it across the canyon and delivered the pizza!

Science and teamwork
saved the day!

YOU DON'T SEE AIR PRESSURE, YOU FEEL IT!

Air pressure is the force applied to a surface by the force of air. Air has weight, and it presses against everything it touches.

In this book the Fix-It Force uses a leaf blower to make it look like Tiny is flying. A leaf blower works by forcing air out at high speed. To deliver a pizza to the other side of Bridgeless Canyon, the team sets up a line of leaf blowers. The pizza floats across the canyon, driven by the air jets of the leaf blowers. Science is cool!